No one like
you

Written by Jillian Harker
Illustrated by Pamela Venus

Bright ☆ Sparks

Ruff was hungry. A huge grumble rumbled around his tummy. He could hear Rufus clattering around in the kitchen. A delicious smell of freshly baked cupcakes sailed past his nose.

"Yummy," thought Ruff.

Ruff skipped into the kitchen – Rufus was tidying up.

"Would you like some help?" asked Ruff. "I could try one of those cupcakes for you."

"Oh, really!" said Rufus, smiling.

"No one makes cup cakes like you," said Ruff

Ruff was bored. He twiddled his
fingers, tapped his toes and twiddled his
fingers again. He had no one to play with.

Later, Ruff tiptoed back into the living room – Rufus was reading.

"Would you like something better to read?" asked Ruff. "I could find you an exciting story."

"Oh, really!" said Rufus, smiling.

"No one tells a story like you," said Ruff.

Ruff was annoyed. He was trying to make a model car. He fiddled and twiddled and fiddled, but he couldn't put it together.

Then he had an idea!

Ruff galloped out to the garden–Rufus was working.

"Would you like something fun to do?" asked Ruff.
"I could let you help me with my model car."

"Oh, really!" said Rufus, smiling.

"No one's as much fun as you,"
said Ruff.

It was bedtime! Rufus tucked Ruff into bed.

Ruff was feeling scared. He didn't like the shadows that flickered all round—it was very quiet.

Then he had an idea!

Ruff crept out of his bedroom and into Rufus's room.

Rufus was snoring loudly. It made Ruff giggle and woke Rufus up.

"Would you like someone to cuddle?" asked Ruff. "I'm very good at cuddling."

"Oh, really!" said Rufus, smiling.

"No one cuddles quite like you,"

yawned Ruff, climbing into
Rufus's bed.

"Oh, really!" said Rufus…

"Well, no one loves you quite as much as I do,
because there's no one like you."

F. Venus